HAL•LEONARD

JAZZ PLAY ALONG

ok and CD for B♭, E♭ and C Instruments

Arranged and Produced by
Mark Taylor

Great
STAN

10 Jazz Standards

HAL LEONARD EUROPE
DISTRIBUTED BY MUSIC SALES

Exclusive Distributors:
Music Sales Limited
8/9 Frith Street, London W1D 3JB, England.

Order No. HLE90002352
ISBN 1-84449-840-9
This book © Copyright 2005 by Hal Leonard Europe

Printed in the USA

Your Guarantee of Quality
As publishers, we strive to produce every book to the highest commercial standards.
This book has been carefully designed to minimise awkward page turns and to make playing from it a real pleasure.
Throughout, the printing and binding have been planned to ensure a sturdy, attractive publication which should give years of enjoyment.
If your copy fails to meet our high standards, please inform us and we will gladly replace it.

www.musicsales.com

Great Jazz Standards

Arranged and Produced by
Mark Taylor

Featured Players:

Graham Breedlove-Trumpet
John Desalme-Tenor Sax
Tony Nalker-Piano
Jim Roberts and Paul Henry-Bass
Steve Fidyk-Drums

HOW TO USE THE CD:

Each song has <u>two</u> tracks:

1) Split Track/Melody

Woodwind, Brass, Keyboard, and Mallet Players can use this track as a learning tool for melody style and inflection.

Bass Players can learn and perform with this track – remove the recorded bass track by turning down the volume on the LEFT channel.

Keyboard and **Guitar Players** can learn and perform with this track – remove the recorded piano part by turning down the volume on the RIGHT channel.

2) Full Stereo Track

Soloists or **groups** can learn and perform with this accompaniment track with the RHYTHM SECTION only.

CALL ME IRRESPONSIBLE
FROM THE PARAMOUNT PICTURE PAPA'S DELICATE CONDITION

WORDS BY SAMMY CAHN
MUSIC BY JAMES VAN HEUSEN

FLY ME TO THE MOON
(IN OTHER WORDS)

WORDS AND MUSIC BY
BART HOWARD

◆3: SPLIT TRACK/MELODY
◆4: FULL STEREO TRACK

C VERSION

HONEYSUCKLE ROSE

WORDS BY ANDY RAZAF
MUSIC BY THOMAS "FATS" WALLER

C VERSION

GIRL TALK
FROM THE PARAMOUNT PICTURE HARLOW

WORDS BY BOBBY TROUP
MUSIC BY NEAL HEFTI

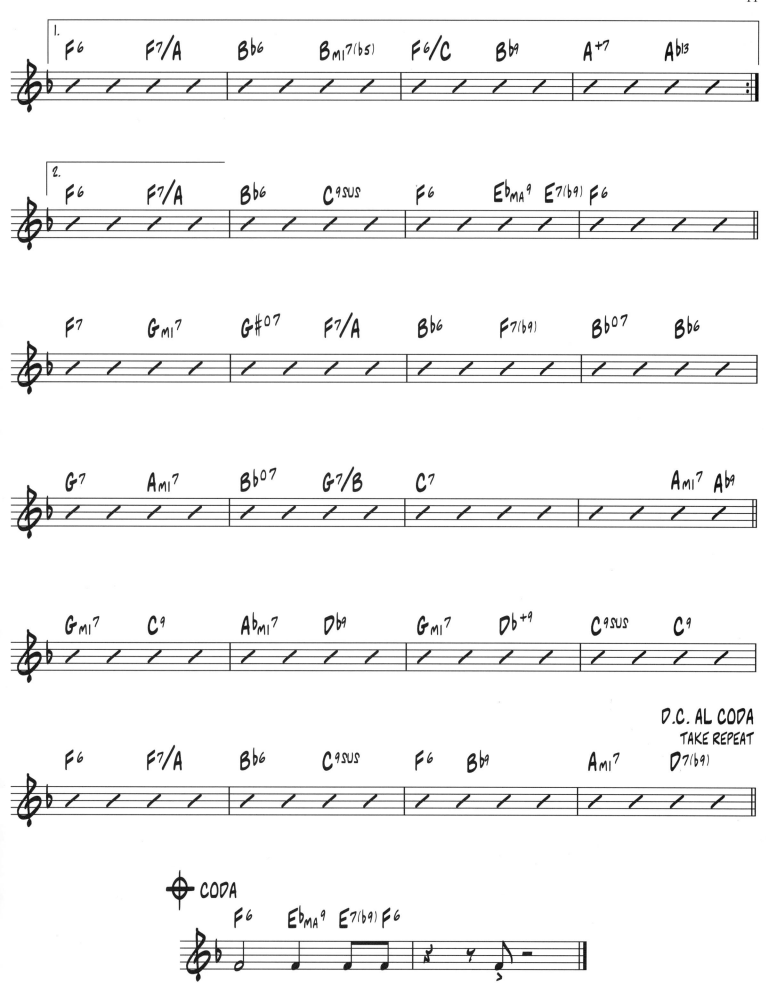

I'LL REMEMBER APRIL

WORDS AND MUSIC BY PAT JOHNSON,
DON RAYE AND GENE DE PAUL

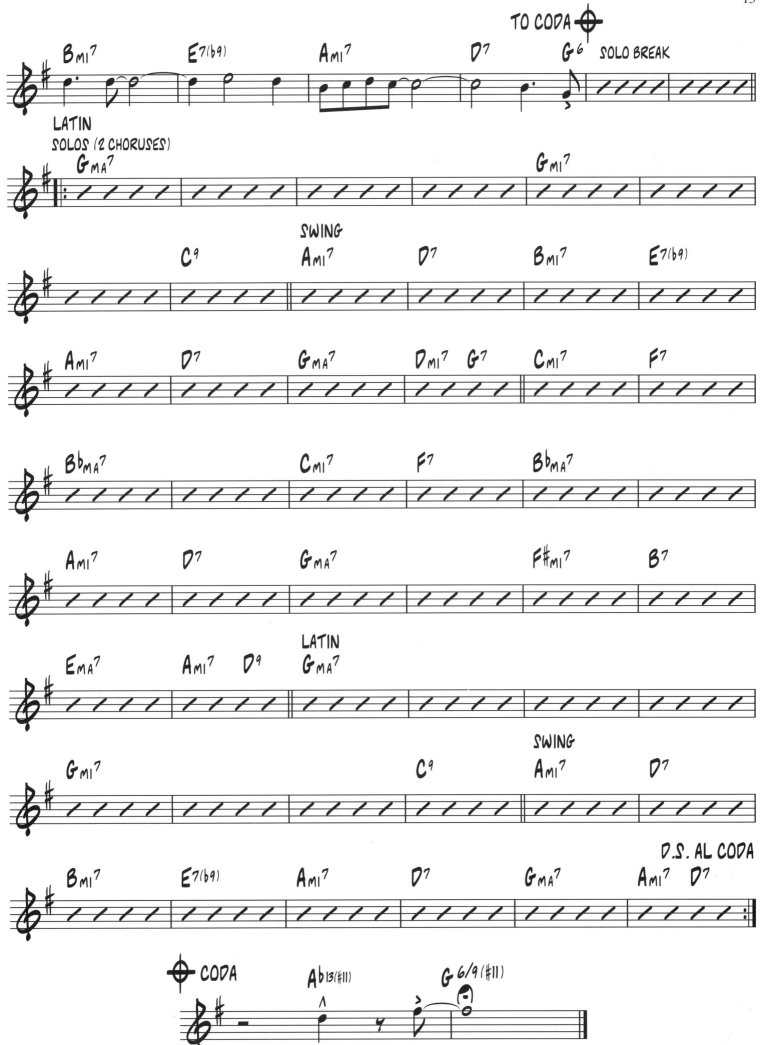

IT COULD HAPPEN TO YOU

FROM THE PARAMOUNT PICTURE AND THE ANGELS SING

WORDS BY JOHNNY BURKE
MUSIC BY JAMES VAN HEUSEN

C VERSION

MEDIUM SWING

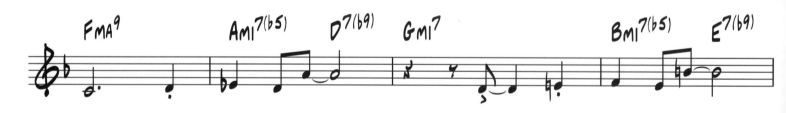

LOVER
FROM THE PARAMOUNT PICTURE LOVE ME TONIGHT

WORDS BY LORENZ HART
MUSIC BY RICHARD RODGERS

SOFTLY AS IN A MORNING SUNRISE

WORDS BY SIGMUND ROMBERG
MUSIC BY O. HAMMERSTEIN II

C VERSION

CD
15: SPLIT TRACK/MELODY
16: FULL STEREO TRACK

18

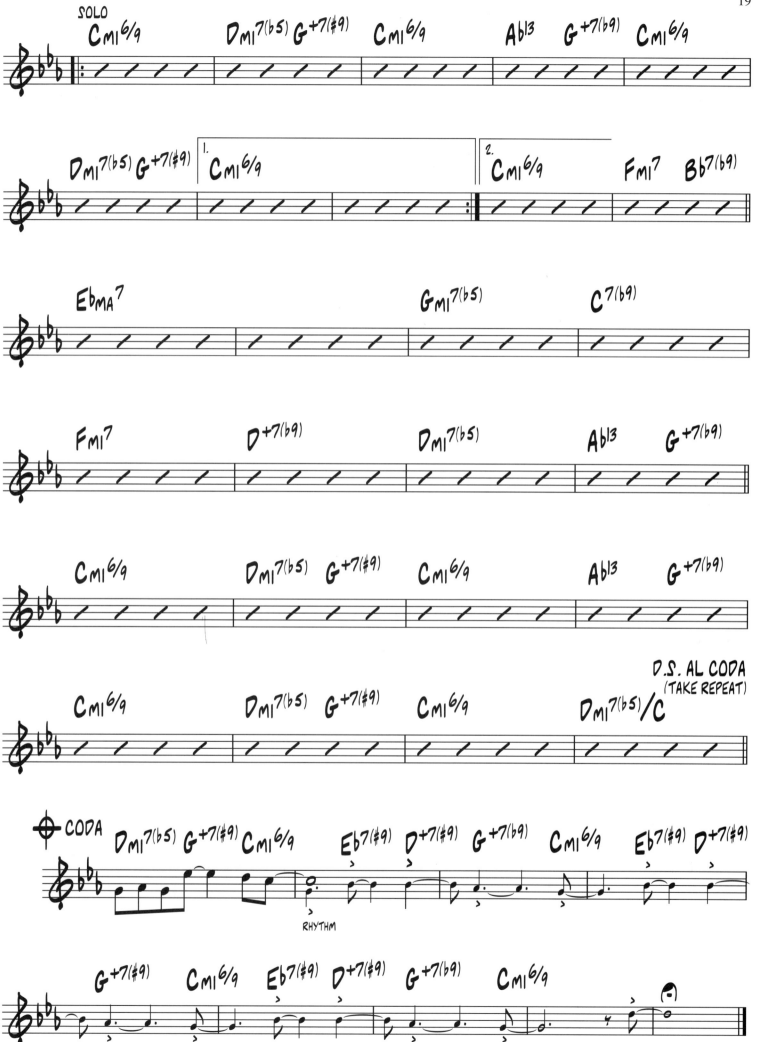

TANGERINE

FROM THE PARAMOUNT PICTURE THE FLEET'S IN

WORDS BY JOHNNY MERCER
MUSIC BY VICTOR SCHERTZINGER

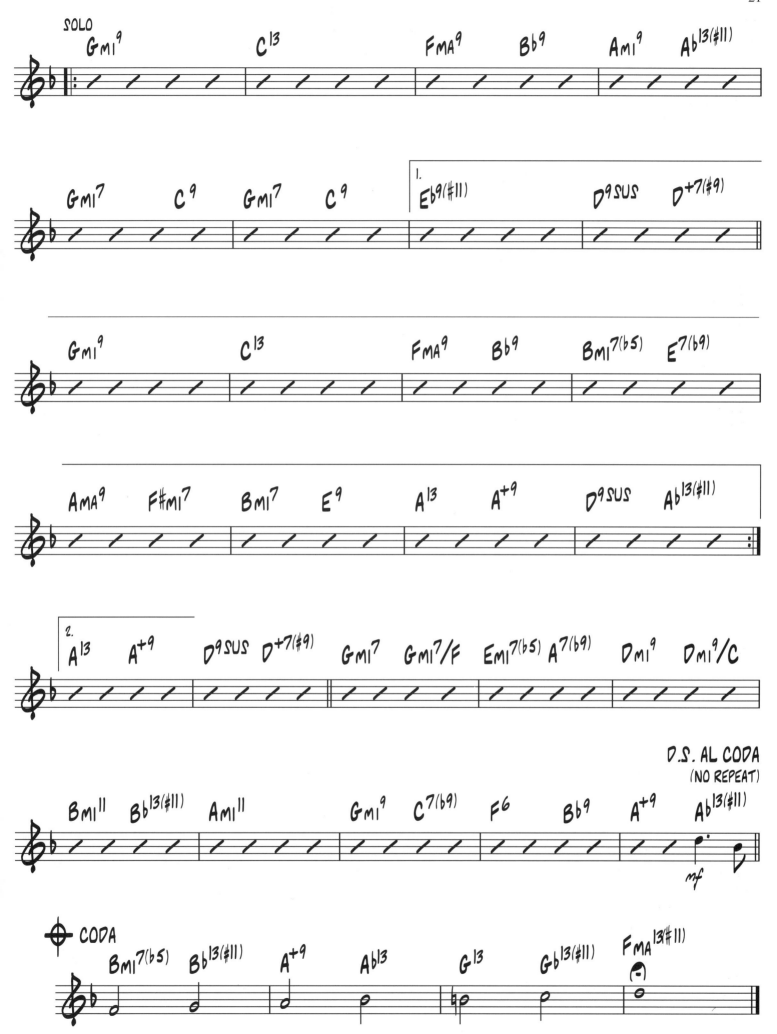

THERE IS NO GREATER LOVE

CD
◆ 19 : SPLIT TRACK/MELODY
◆ 20 : FULL STEREO TRACK

WORDS BY MARTY SYMES
MUSIC BY ISHAM JONES

C VERSION

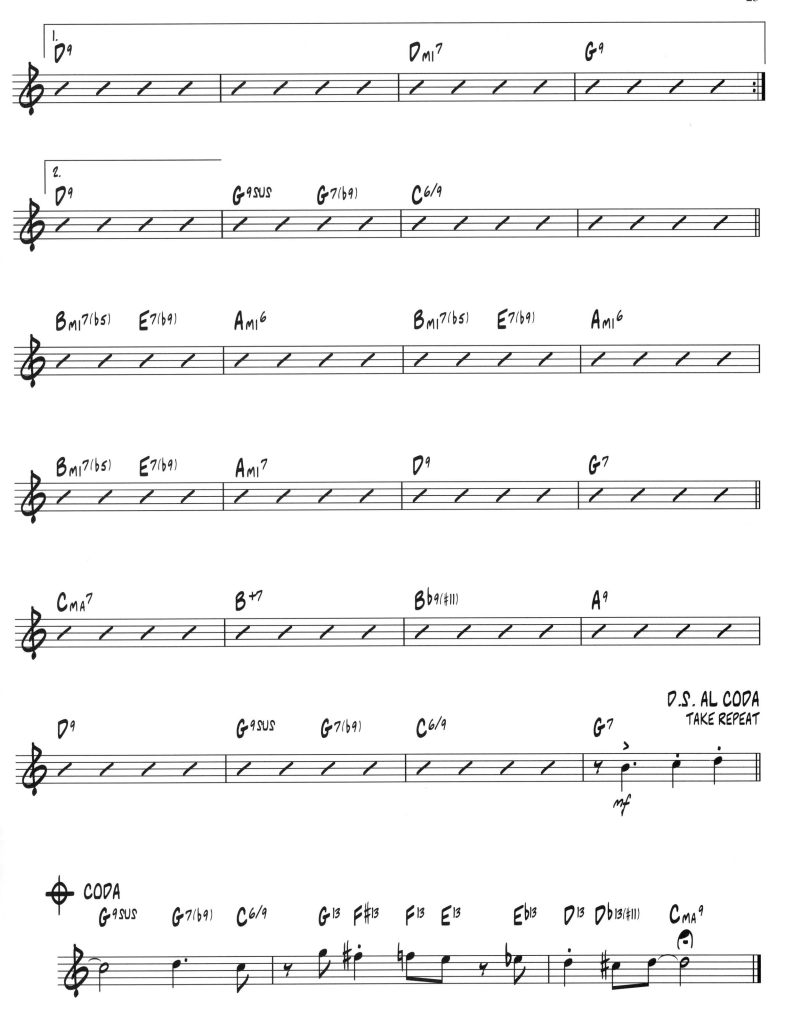

GIRL TALK
FROM THE PARAMOUNT PICTURE HARLOW

WORDS BY BOBBY TROUP
MUSIC BY NEAL HEFTI

B♭ LEAD SHEETS

CD
1 : SPLIT TRACK/MELODY
2 : FULL STEREO TRACK

CALL ME IRRESPONSIBLE
FROM THE PARAMOUNT PICTURE PAPA'S DELICATE CONDITION

WORDS BY SAMMY CAHN
MUSIC BY JAMES VAN HEUSEN

Bb VERSION

FLY ME TO THE MOON
(IN OTHER WORDS)

WORDS AND MUSIC BY
BART HOWARD

HONEYSUCKLE ROSE

I'LL REMEMBER APRIL

WORDS AND MUSIC BY PAT JOHNSON,
DON RAYE AND GENE DE PAUL

Bb VERSION

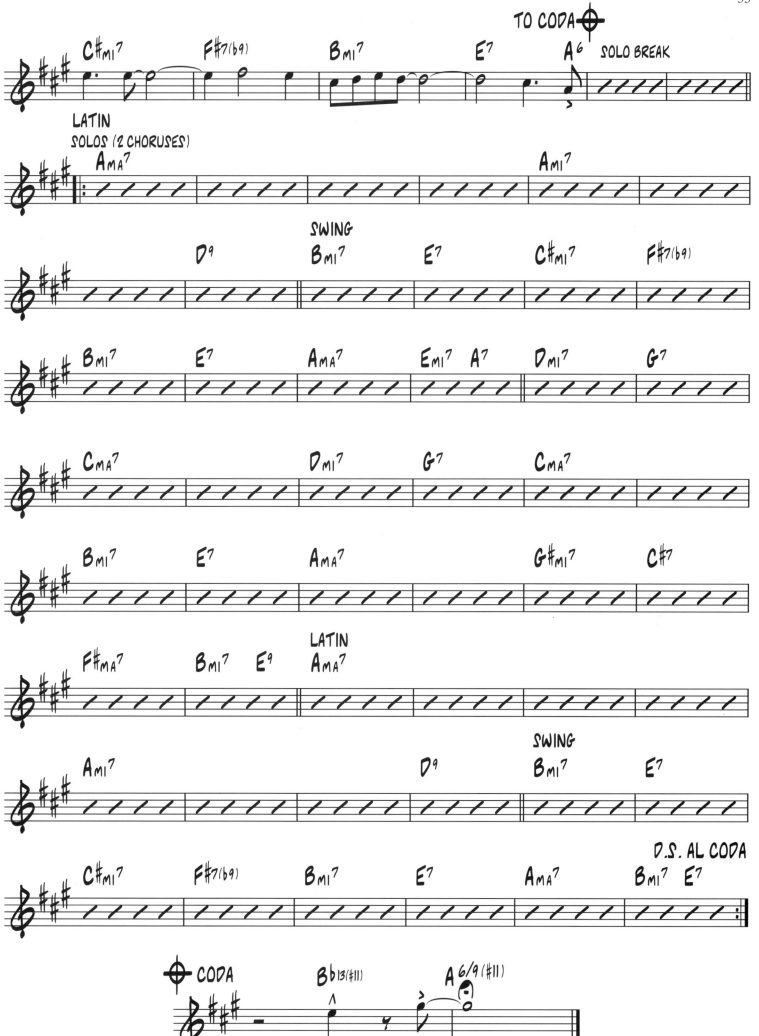

IT COULD HAPPEN TO YOU

FROM THE PARAMOUNT PICTURE AND THE ANGELS SING

WORDS BY JOHNNY BURKE
MUSIC BY JAMES VAN HEUSEN

LOVER
FROM THE PARAMOUNT PICTURE LOVE ME TONIGHT

WORDS BY LORENZ HART
MUSIC BY RICHARD RODGERS

SOFTLY AS IN A MORNING SUNRISE

WORDS BY SIGMUND ROMBERG
MUSIC BY O. HAMMERSTEIN II

CD
15 : SPLIT TRACK/MELODY
16 : FULL STEREO TRACK

TANGERINE
FROM THE PARAMOUNT PICTURE THE FLEET'S IN

WORDS BY JOHNNY MERCER
MUSIC BY VICTOR SCHERTZINGER

17 : SPLIT TRACK/MELODY
18 : FULL STEREO TRACK

Bb VERSION

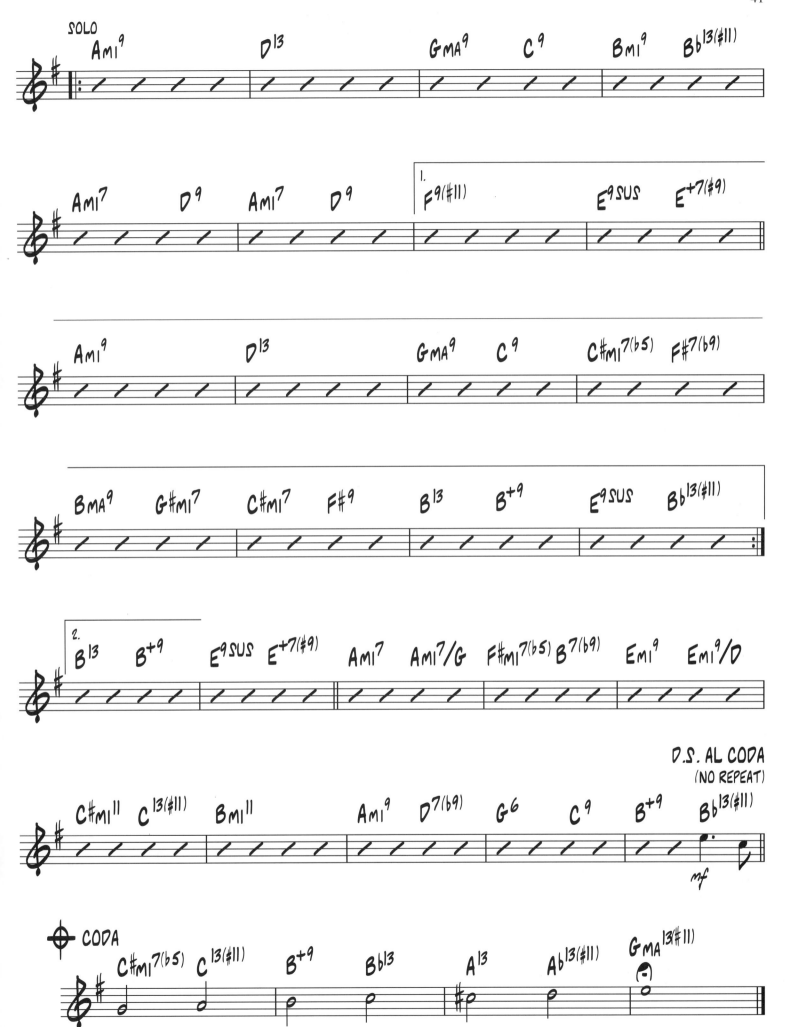

THERE IS NO GREATER LOVE

WORDS BY MARTY SYMES
MUSIC BY ISHAM JONES

GIRL TALK
FROM THE PARAMOUNT PICTURE HARLOW

WORDS BY BOBBY TROUP
MUSIC BY NEAL HEFTI

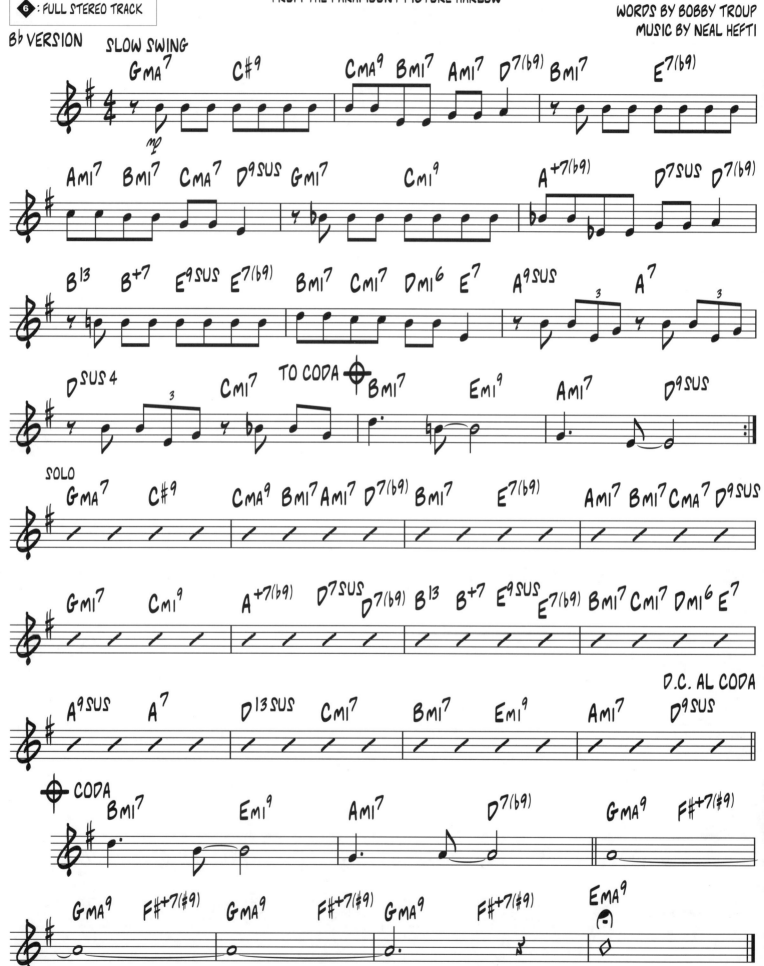

E♭ LEAD SHEETS

CALL ME IRRESPONSIBLE

FROM THE PARAMOUNT PICTURE PAPA'S DELICATE CONDITION

WORDS BY SAMMY CAHN
MUSIC BY JAMES VAN HEUSEN

FLY ME TO THE MOON
(IN OTHER WORDS)

WORDS AND MUSIC BY
BART HOWARD

◆3 : SPLIT TRACK/MELODY
◆4 : FULL STEREO TRACK

Eb VERSION

HONEYSUCKLE ROSE

I'LL REMEMBER APRIL

CD
◆9 : SPLIT TRACK/MELODY
◆10 : FULL STEREO TRACK

Eb VERSION

WORDS AND MUSIC BY PAT JOHNSON,
DON RAYE AND GENE DE PAUL

E F# G# B C#

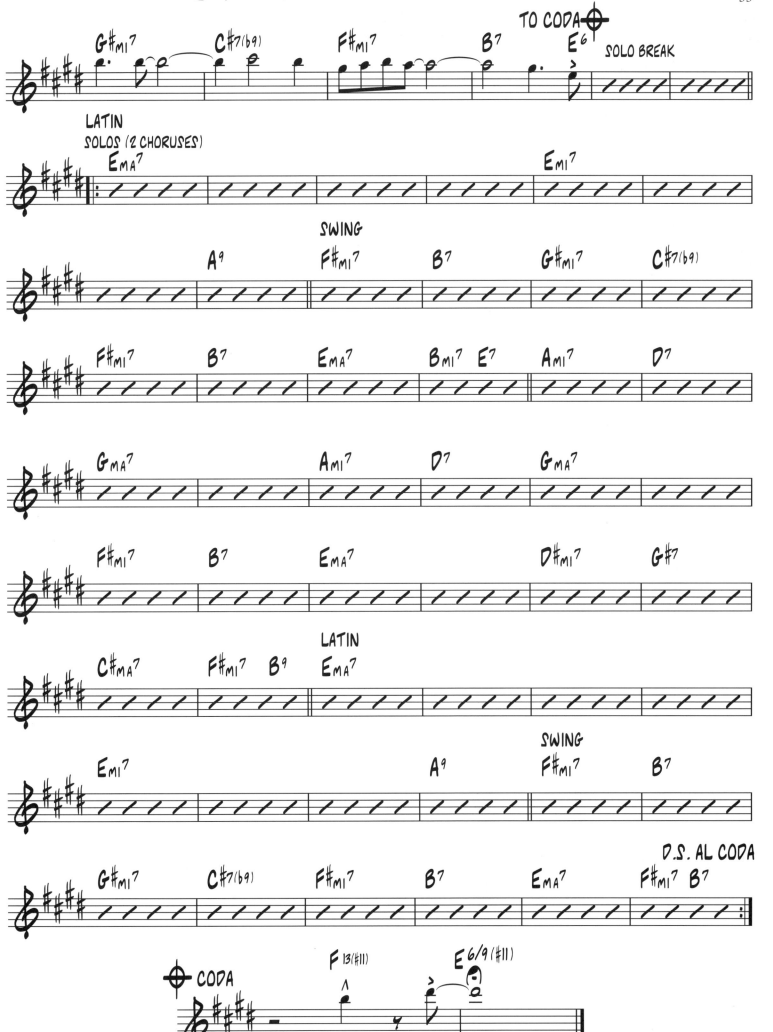

IT COULD HAPPEN TO YOU

FROM THE PARAMOUNT PICTURE AND THE ANGELS SING

WORDS BY JOHNNY BURKE
MUSIC BY JAMES VAN HEUSEN

Eb VERSION

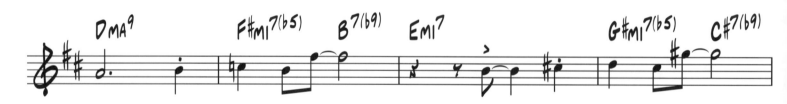

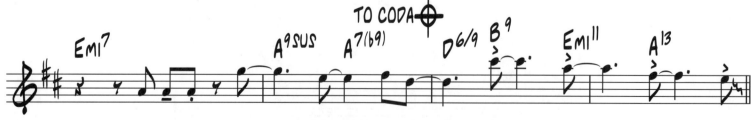

LOVER
FROM THE PARAMOUNT PICTURE LOVE ME TONIGHT

WORDS BY LORENZ HART
MUSIC BY RICHARD RODGERS

SOFTLY AS IN A MORNING SUNRISE

WORDS BY SIGMUND ROMBERG
MUSIC BY O. HAMMERSTEIN II

TANGERINE
FROM THE PARAMOUNT PICTURE THE FLEET'S IN

WORDS BY JOHNNY MERCER
MUSIC BY VICTOR SCHERTZINGER

E♭ VERSION

D E F# A B

THERE IS NO GREATER LOVE

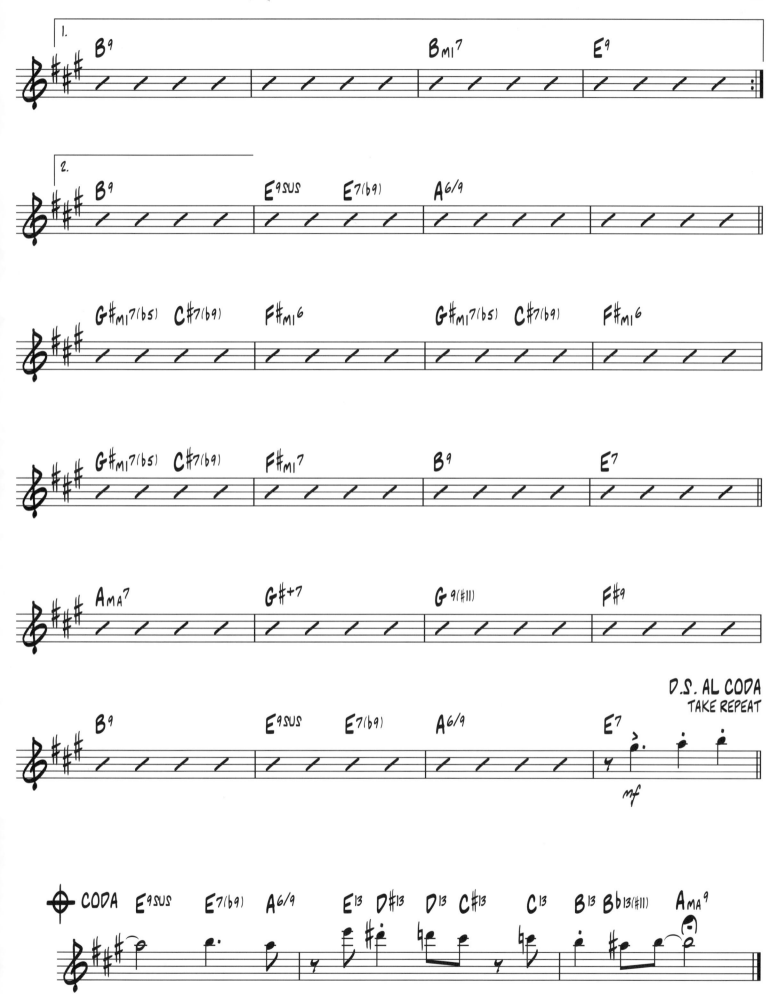

GIRL TALK
FROM THE PARAMOUNT PICTURE HARLOW

WORDS BY BOBBY TROUP
MUSIC BY NEAL HEFTI

𝄢 C LEAD SHEETS

CALL ME IRRESPONSIBLE

FROM THE PARAMOUNT PICTURE PAPA'S DELICATE CONDITION

WORDS BY SAMMY CAHN
MUSIC BY JAMES VAN HEUSEN

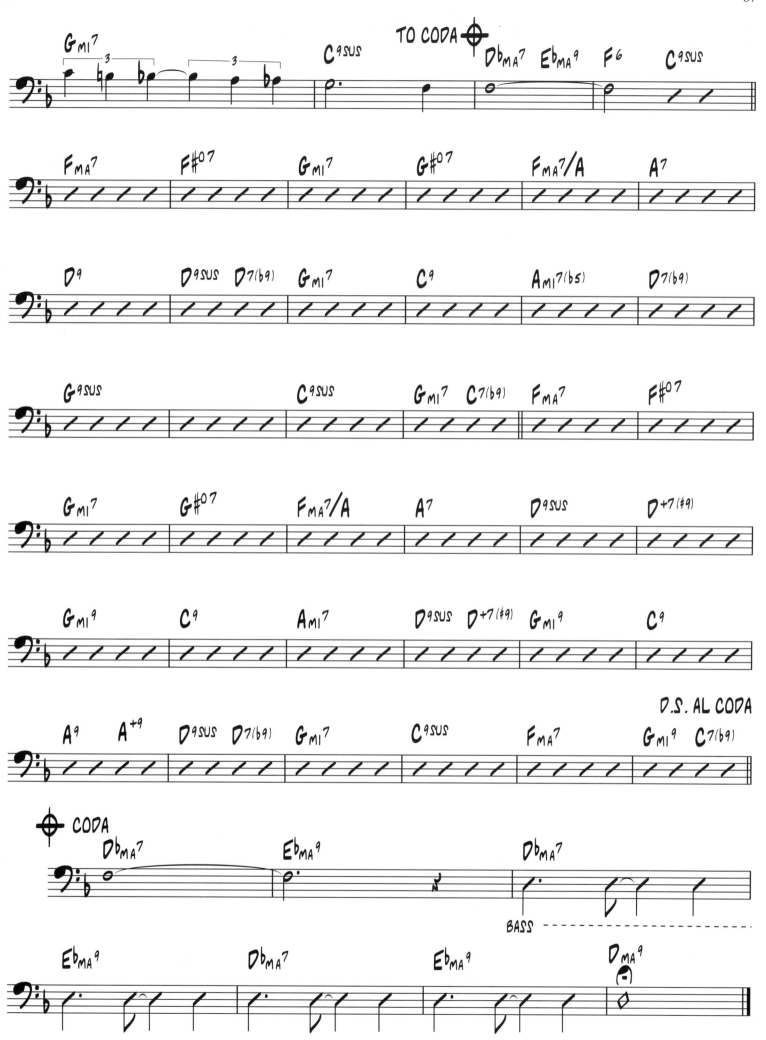

FLY ME TO THE MOON
(IN OTHER WORDS)

WORDS AND MUSIC BY
BART HOWARD

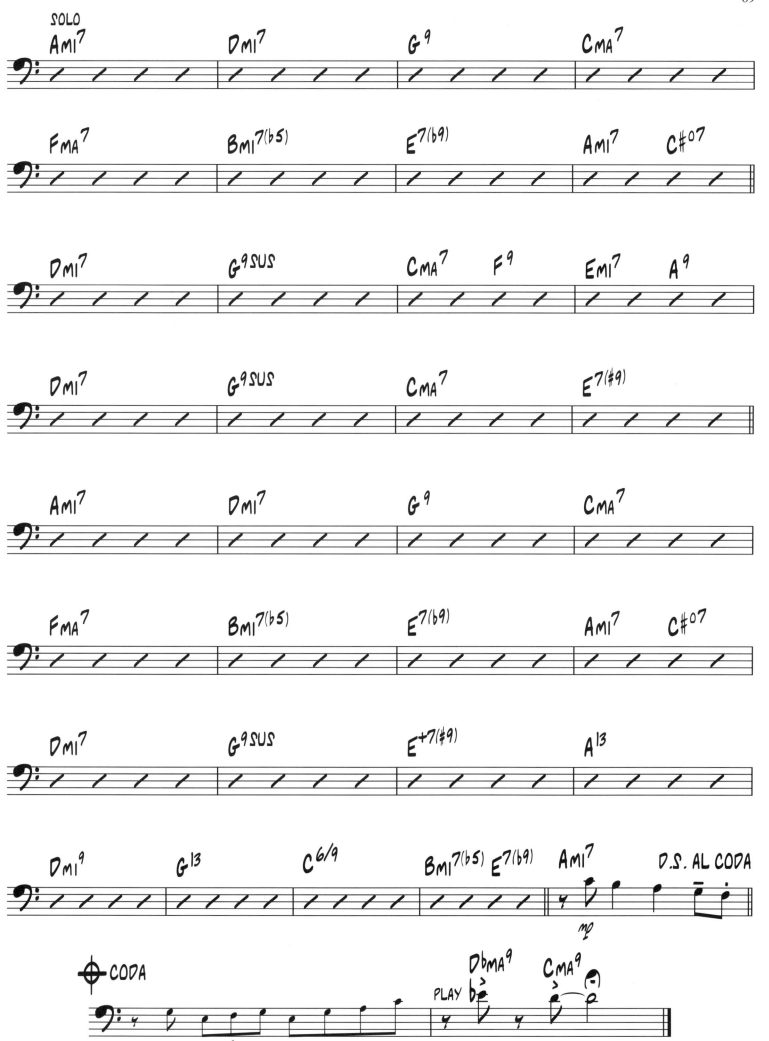

HONEYSUCKLE ROSE

WORDS BY ANDY RAZAF
MUSIC BY THOMAS "FATS" WALLER

I'LL REMEMBER APRIL

WORDS AND MUSIC BY PAT JOHNSON,
DON RAYE AND GENE DE PAUL

CD
- **9** : SPLIT TRACK/MELODY
- **10** : FULL STEREO TRACK

C VERSION

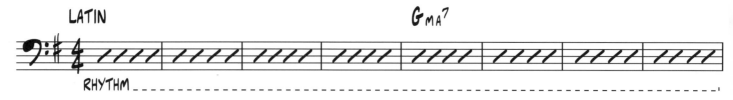

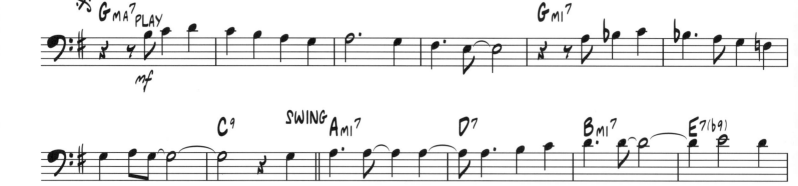

IT COULD HAPPEN TO YOU
FROM THE PARAMOUNT PICTURE AND THE ANGELS SING

WORDS BY JOHNNY BURKE
MUSIC BY JAMES VAN HEUSEN

LOVER
FROM THE PARAMOUNT PICTURE LOVE ME TONIGHT

WORDS BY LORENZ HART
MUSIC BY RICHARD RODGERS

SOFTLY AS IN A MORNING SUNRISE

WORDS BY SIGMUND ROMBERG
MUSIC BY O. HAMMERSTEIN II

TANGERINE
FROM THE PARAMOUNT PICTURE THE FLEET'S IN

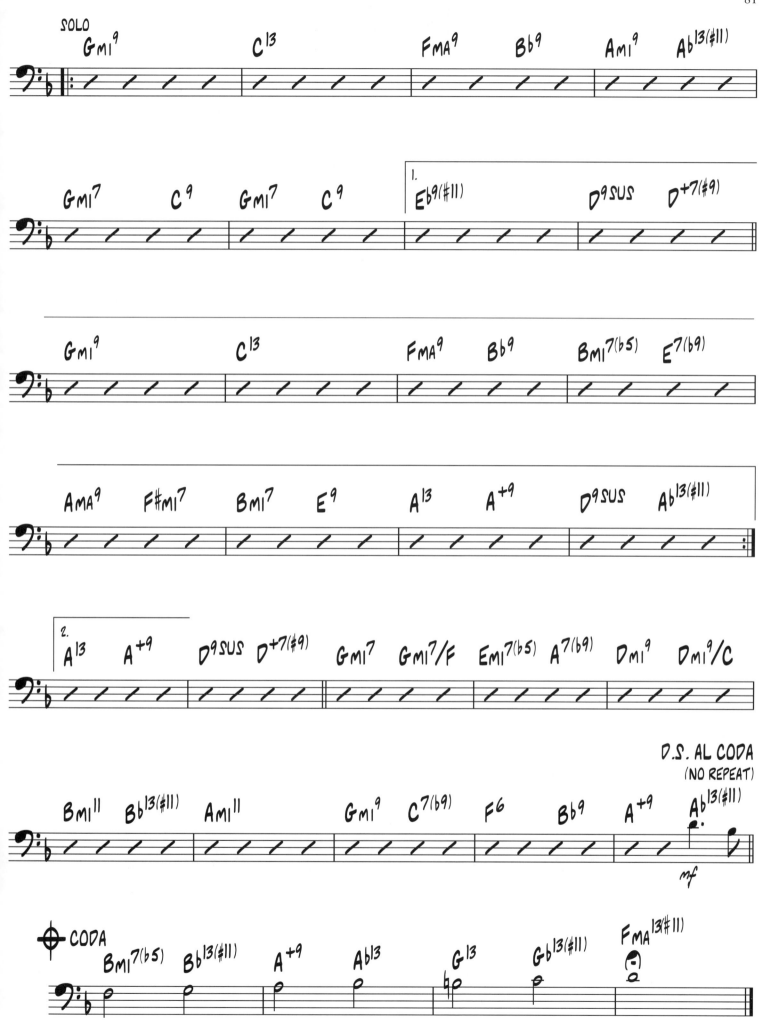

THERE IS NO GREATER LOVE

WORDS BY MARTY SYMES
MUSIC BY ISHAM JONES

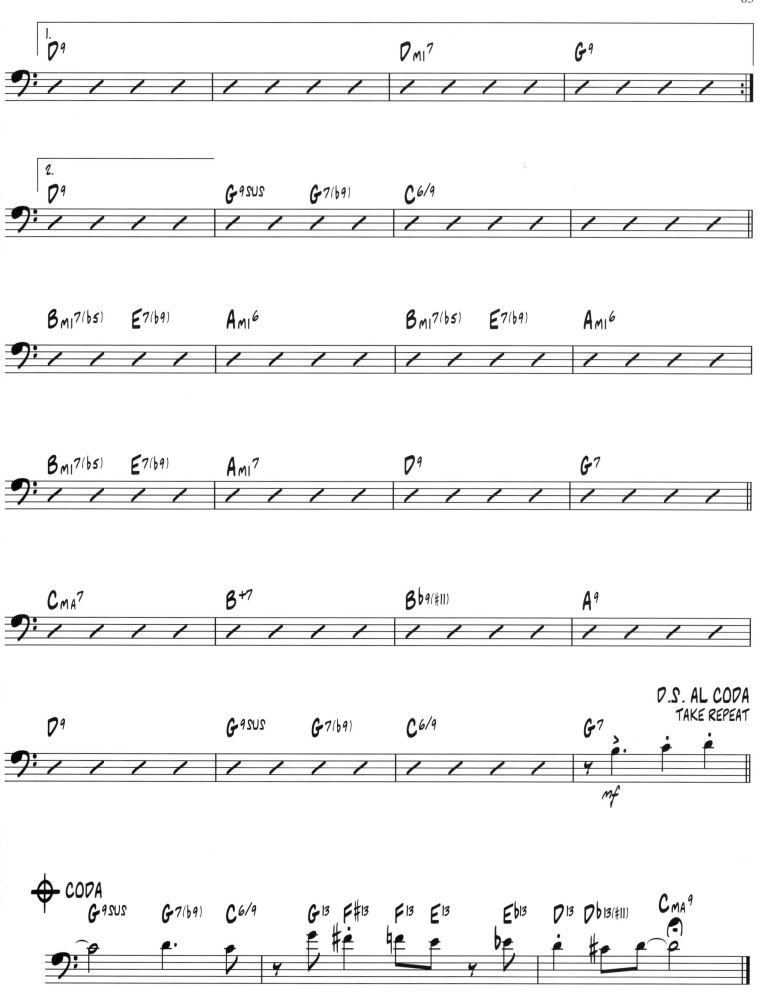

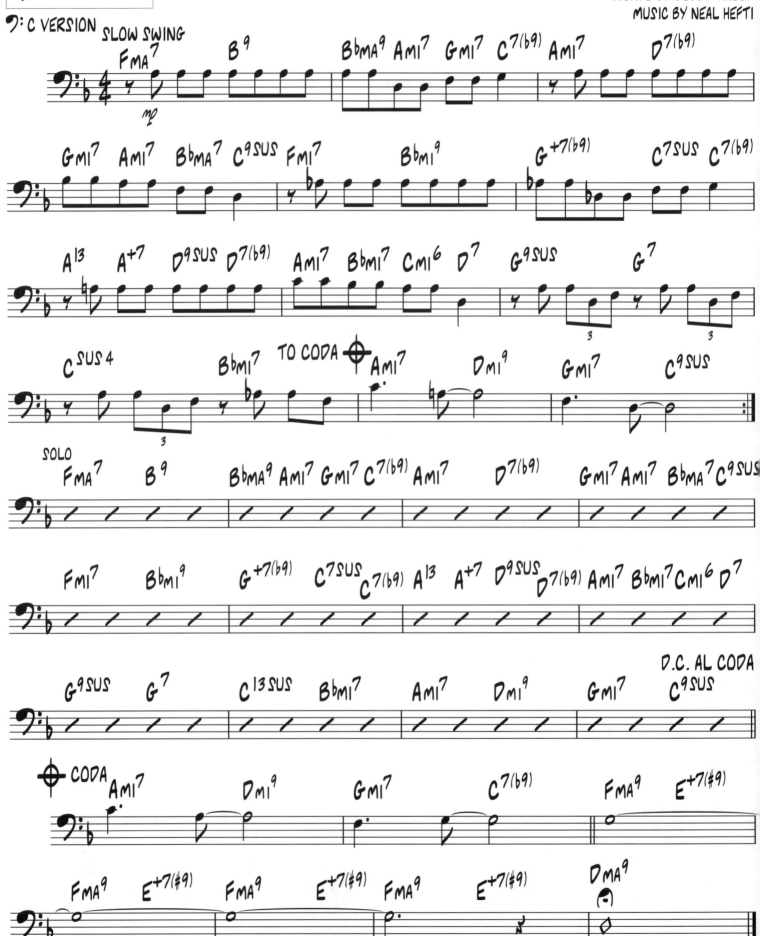

GIRL TALK
FROM THE PARAMOUNT PICTURE HARLOW

WORDS BY BOBBY TROUP
MUSIC BY NEAL HEFTI

LYRICS

Lyrics

CALL ME IRRESPONSIBLE

Call me irresponsible, call me unreliable,
Throw in undependable too.
Do my foolish alibis bore you?
Well, I'm not too clever.
I just adore you.

Call me unpredictable, tell me I'm impractical
Rainbows I'm inclined to pursue.
Call me irresponsible, yes, I'm unreliable,
But it's undeniably true,
I'm irresponsibly mad for you!

FLY ME TO THE MOON
(IN OTHER WORDS)

Fly me to the moon,
And let me play among the stars;
Let me see what spring is like
On Jupiter and Mars.
In other words, hold my hand!
In other words, darling, kiss me!

Fill my heart with song,
And let me sing forever more;
You are all I long for,
All I worship and adore.
In other words, please be true.
In other words, I love you!

GIRL TALK

They like to chat about the dresses they will wear tonight,
They chew the fat about their tresses and the neighbors' fight;
Inconsequential things that men don't really care to know,
become essential things that women find so "appropo."
But that's a dame, they're all the same; it's just a game.
They call it girl talk, girl talk.

They all meow about the ups and downs for all their friends,
The "who,", the "how," the "why," they dish the dirt, it never ends,
The weaker sex, the speaker sex we mortal males behold,
But tho' we joke we wouldn't trade you for a ton of gold.

HONEYSUCKLE ROSE

Ev'ry honey bee fills with jealousy
When they see you out with me.
I don't blame them, goodness knows,
Honeysuckle rose.

When you're passin' by, flowers droop and sigh,
And I know the reason why:
You're much sweeter, goodness knows,
Honeysuckle rose.

Don't buy sugar, you just have to touch my cup
You're my sugar, it's sweet when you stir it up.

When I'm takin' sips from your tasty lips,
Seems the honey fairly drips.
You're confection, goodness knows,
Honeysuckle rose.

I'LL REMEMBER APRIL

This lovely day will lengthen into ev'ning.
We'll sign goodbye to all we've ever had.
Alone where we have walked together,
I'll remember April and be glad.

I'll be content you loved me once in April.
Your lips were warm and love and Spring were new.
But I'm not afraid of Autumn and her sorrow,
For I'll remember April and you.

The fire will dwindle into glowing ashes,
For flames and love live such a little while.
I won't forget, but I won't be lonely,
I'll remember April, and I'll smile.

IT COULD HAPPEN TO YOU

Hide your heart from sight,
Lock your dreams at night.
It could happen to you.
Don't count stars or you might stumble,
Someone drops a sigh,
And down you tumble.

Keep an eye on spring,
Run when church bells ring.
It could happen to you.
All I did was wonder
How your arms would be
And it happened to me!

LOVER

Lover, when I'm near you,
And I hear you speak my name
Softly in my ear, you breathe a flame.

Lover, when we're dancing,
Keep on glancing in my eyes
Till love's own entrancing music dies.

All of my future is in you.
Your ev'ry plan I design.
Promise you'll always continue to be mine.

Lover, please be tender.
When you're tender, fears depart.
Lover, I surrender to my heart.

Lover, when I'm near you,
And I hear you speak my name
Softly in my ear, you breathe a flame.

Lover, it's immoral,
But why quarrel with our bliss
When two lips of coral want to kiss?

I say, "The Devil is in you,"
And to resist you I try;
But if you didn't continue, I would die!

Lover, please be tender.
When you're tender, fears depart.
Lover, I surrender to my heart.

SOFTLY AS IN A MORNING SUNRISE

Softly as in a morning sunrise,
The light of love comes stealing
Into a newborn day, oh!

Flaming with all the glow of sunrise,
A burning kiss is sealing
The vow that all betray.

For the passions that thrill love
And lift you high to heaven,
Are the passions that kill love
And let you fall to hell! So ends each story.

Softly as in an evening sunset,
The light that gave you glory
Will take it all away.

TANGERINE

Tangerine, she is all they claim with her eyes of night and lips as bright as flame.
Tangerine, when she dances by Señoritas stare and caballeros sigh.

And I've seen toasts to Tangerine raised in ev'ry bar across the Argentine.
Yes, she has them all on the run but her heart belongs to just one.
Her heart belongs to Tangerine.

THERE IS NO GREATER LOVE

There is no greater love than what I feel for you,
No greater love, no heart so true.
There is no greater thrill than what you bring to me,
No sweeter song than what you sing to me.

You're the sweetest thing I have ever known,
And to think that you are mine alone!
There is no greater love in all the world it's true,
No greater love than what I feel for you.